The Little Duck who lost his fucks

Written and Illustrated by

Julia Green

Julia Green
2018

First Printing: 2018

2nd Edition:2023

ISBN 9798870539898

Julia Green
Poughkeepsie, 12603
www.juliagreenartist.com

Ordering Information
U.S. trade bookstores and wholesalers:
Please contact Julia Green Tel: (850) 712-3818;
email: julia@jgreenaws.com

To my dear friends and family:

Thank you. Without your support, patience and encouragement, this book would not exist.

There once was a wee little duck,

who rose when the sun came up,

but on this fine day,
to his dismay,

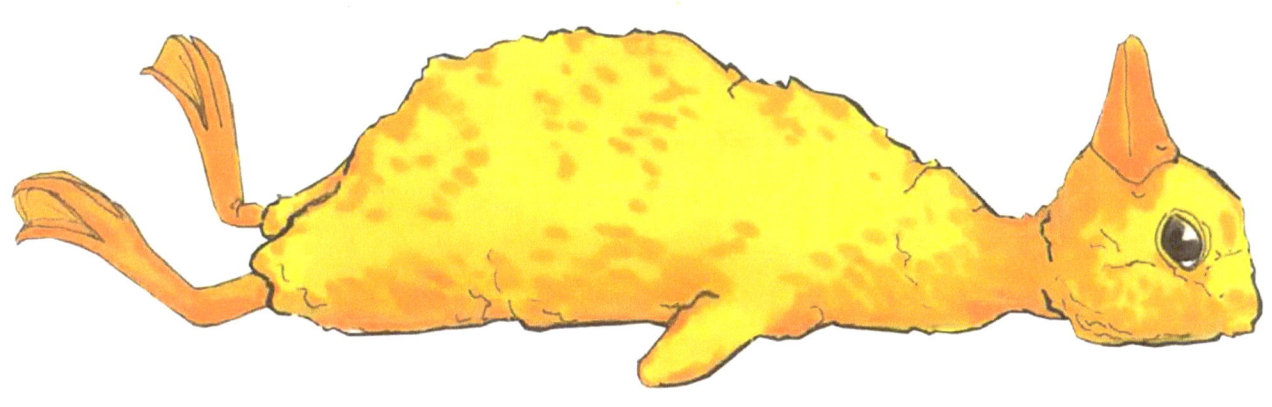

he could not find
his fucks.

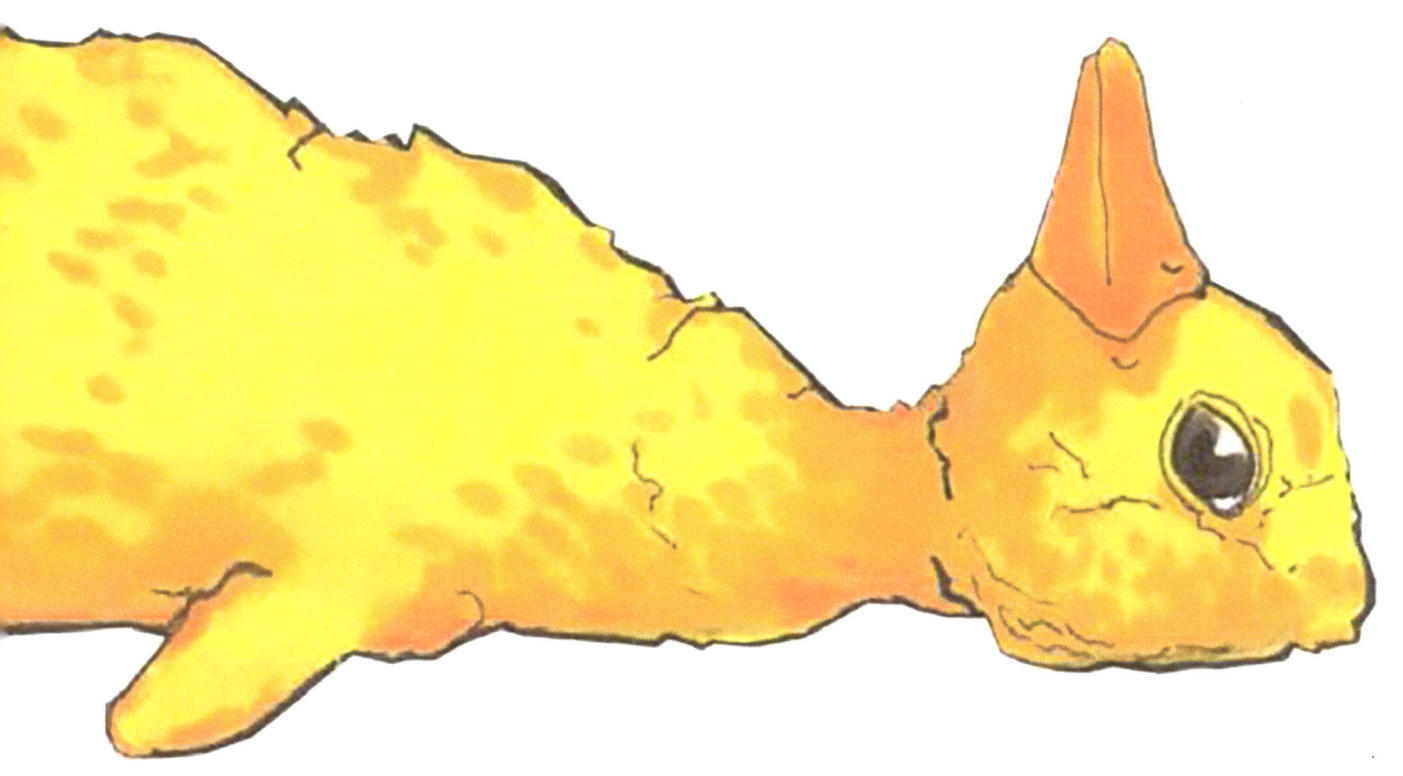

Were his fucks in his jeans?
The washing machine?

Were his fucks on the floor? Inside his drawer?
Next to the shits he had given,
just the day before?

No, Little Duck could
not find his fucks.

"I know what I can do!
exclaimed Little Duck,
"I'll borrow some from a friend!"

He went to the tortoise next door, who had done him some favors before.

Excuse me sir, please pardon the slur,
but could you let me borrow some fucks?

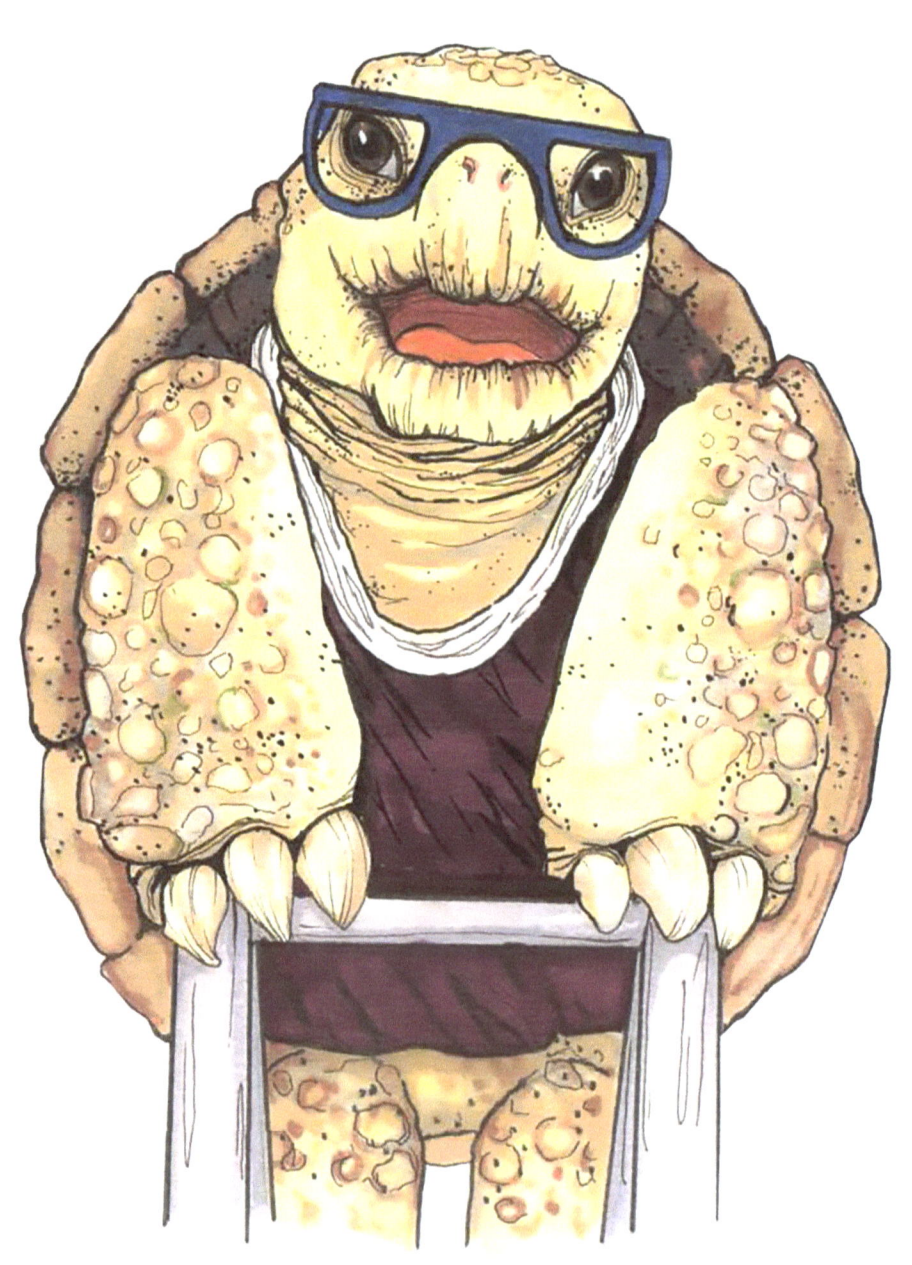

"I'm sorry Little Duck,
I cannot give you my fucks.
In my ripe old age,
I gave them away, many years
before you could cluck."

Next he approached Miss Bunny,
who was frankly,
quite a honey.

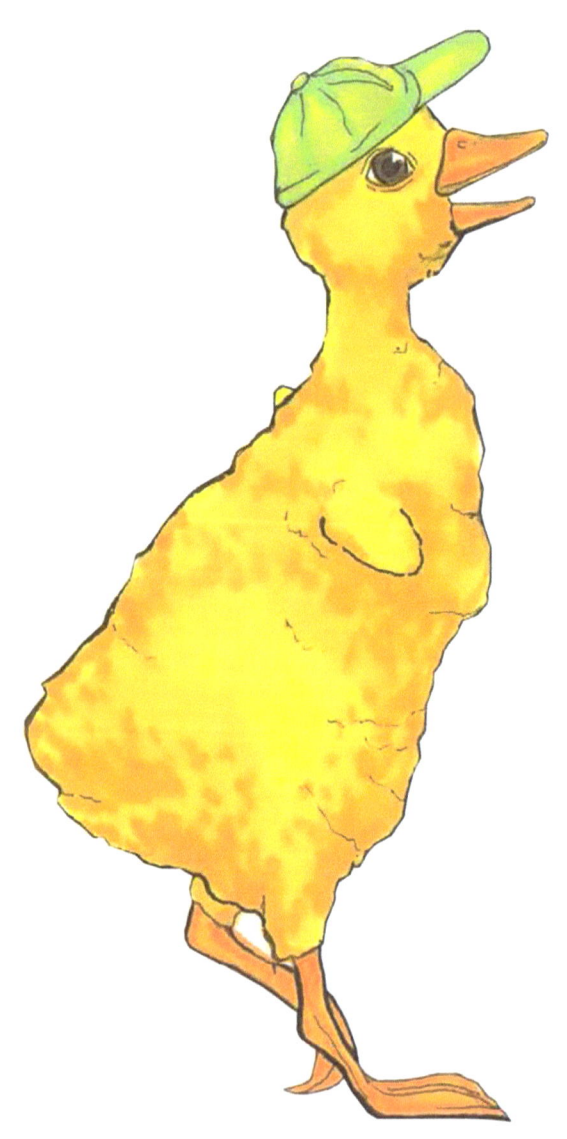

"Excuse me Miss Bunny, this sounds kinda funny, but could you let me borrow some fucks?"

"I'm sorry Little Duck,
I cannot give you my fucks. I gave them
away many times just today..."

"Literally."

He asked the old crane on the
bright weather vane.

He asked the raccoons
outside the saloon.

He asked all the pansies-
they said nothing and stared.

He asked the old dog in the big rocking chair.

No one had any fucks to give.

Little Duck had grown
cold, weary and sad.
He took refuge on a
soft lily pad.

When out of the bog came a big green
frog, who looked like he had, just a
tad...of fucks, that is.

"Excuse me sir,
I'm feeling quite stuck,
because I'm just a duck
without any fucks.
Can you help me?"

"No I will not you spoiled little twat!"

"Where have yours gone?! Did you give it some thought?"

"So, you don't give a fuck, and "meaninglessness" sucks; but who's driving this bus? Quit passing the buck duck!"

"Fucks must be selective, not given on a platter. Only give a fuck about things that truly matter!"

"Find the thing that inspires a
boatload of fucks! Time to strut
your cluckin' duck butt
right out of its rut!"

"Strap on your britches! Keep
your chin held high!
At least give a fuck about doing
something worthwhile."

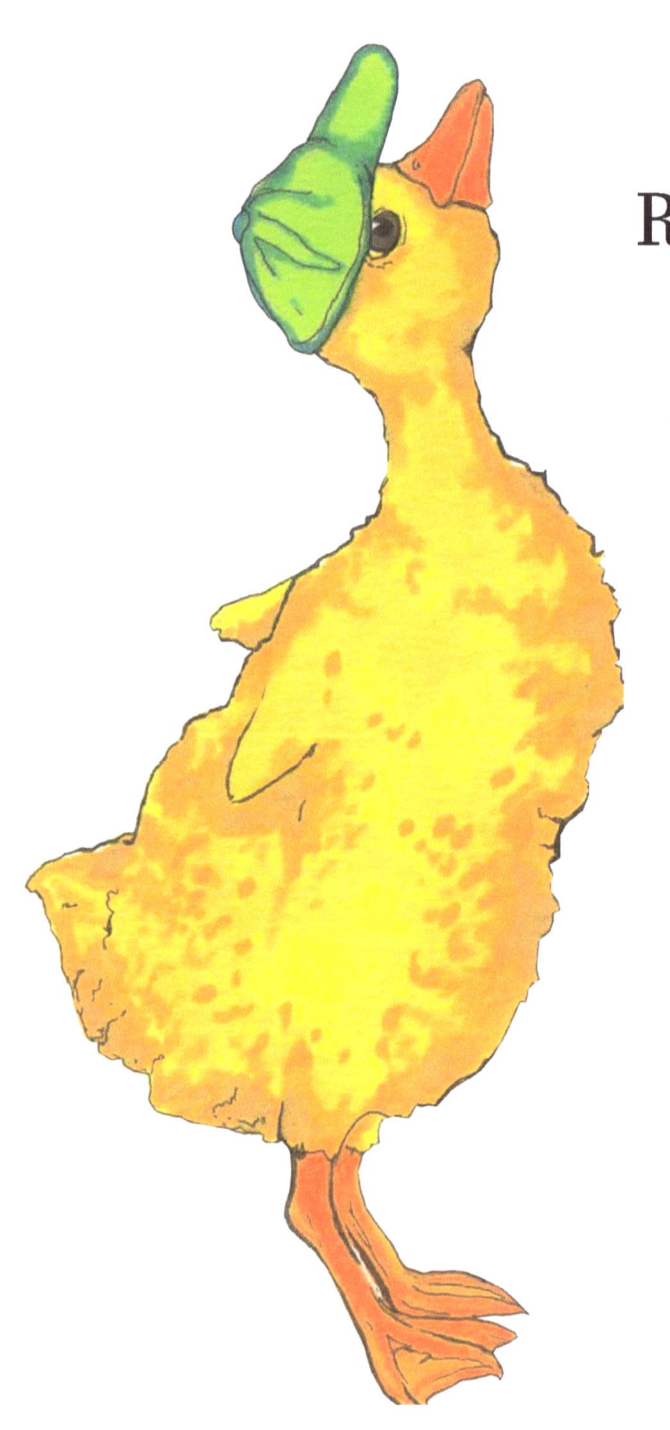

Right at that moment,
the duck mystified,
a little blue fuck fell
from the sky.

It drifted like a
feather, right into
his hands.

"I give a fuck!"he yelled.
"I understand!"

He took his one fuck and
went forth with a smile. One
fuck was enough to find a
passion worthwhile.

In his search for fuckworthiness,
Frog wished him the best,
and felt something growing
in the middle of his chest.

One, tiny fuck had
grown in his heart,
for the brave Little Duck,
and his fresh new start.

THE END